A Happy Christmas for Mr Mole

Written & Illustrated by Peggy Burton

© THE MEDICI SOCIETY LTD · LONDON · 1995   Printed in England   ISBN 0 85503 146 8

Mr Mouse hurried along the edge of the noisy motor-way to his front door hidden in the grassy bank. He rushed into his family waving a letter. 'I have just met the postman,' he panted. 'Marvellous news ! We are moving to Woody Bank — my sister has found us a house near where she lives.'

Mrs Mouse and the children, Timothy, Sally, and little Millie were delighted. 'Great!' said Timothy. 'I can go exploring with cousin Thomas.' They spent the rest of the day packing everything and early next morning they started on their journey.

Pa had a wheelbarrow piled high with furniture. Mrs Mouse pushed the pram with their clothes and some food for when they arrived, and the children pulled a cart with all their belongings. Pa was very happy as he led them towards their new home.

3

They sang as they went along and after a while they came to a wood; the leaves were a beautiful autumn gold. Mrs Mouse was pleased to know they would be settled in before Christmas.

They followed a stream until they came to a notice which read 'HOUSE FOR SALE', and in big red letters across it 'SOLD TO MR MOUSE'.

'How about that?' said Pa. 'It's lovely,' said his wife.

Aunt and Uncle Mouse and Thomas were there to welcome them and they all decided to meet the next day. Thomas stayed behind to help Pa and Timothy unpack while Mrs Mouse and Sally prepared some food because they were all hungry and tired after their journey.

'Who lives in that house across the stream?' asked Timothy. 'Old Mr Mole lives there,' said Thomas. 'He's a bit of a misery and he will chase you away if you go near his house.'

5

Little Millie Mouse had been so excited that she hardly slept a wink and early next morning, while the others were still asleep, she crept outside and had fun dancing in the long grass and rustling through the fallen leaves.

It wasn't long before she was quite lost and tired and she lay down under a toadstool and fell fast asleep.

'What a dear little mouse,' said Susie Squirrel, who was out collecting nuts with brother Sammy. 'I wonder where she lives.' 'I know,' said Jenny Wren, who had landed beside them with Robin. 'She's from the new house; the family moved in yesterday.'

They woke Millie gently and took her home. 'Thank you for bringing her back,' said Mrs Mouse. 'We are new here and we only know Thomas and his parents.' 'But we have lots of friends you must meet,' said Sammy.

Winter was settling in and the Mouse family were very happy.

One day Timothy and Thomas walked across the stepping stones and went quietly past Mr Mole's house.

Exploring further along the bank, they heard music coming from a small opening in the ground. They squeezed through the little hole and found themselves in a dark tunnel with a light at the other end. They crept towards it and came to a lovely room and there at a piano was Mr Mole playing beautiful music.

He was furious when he saw them and shouted, 'How dare you come into my house !' The frightened boys dashed back into the open where they met Mr Squirrel and Sammy walking by the stream.

'How strange,' said Mr Squirrel when he heard what had happened. 'But you mustn't pester Mr Mole, because he is very sad and lonely since his wife died.'

Mr Mole scratched his head. 'It's a mystery,' he thought. 'I've checked the door and windows and I still wonder how those boys got in.'

Back in his room he felt it was getting much, much colder. So he decided that the best place to be was in his cosy bed. He filled a hot water bottle, put extra rugs on the bed, and was soon tucked up reading one of his favourite books.

He woke next morning to the sounds of laughter and lots of noise. When he looked out, he saw the ground was white with frost and snow and the stream was a sheet of ice — and there, right near his front door, were crowds of youngsters, skating, sliding and having fun.

He quickly put on his warm coat and went outside. 'Get away from my house !' he shouted. 'Go and play somewhere else.'

13

That evening a gale blew up and the animals huddled together listening as things crashed down outside.

Timothy Mouse woke the next morning to a loud banging and there at the door was Uncle Mouse with Squirrel, Rabbit and young Thomas.

'Quickly! Get your Pa,' panted Uncle. 'A big branch has smashed into Mole's front door. 'We'd better see if he's all right — and bring some rope with you.' 'I'll go with Tom,' said Timothy. 'We know a way in.'

So, while the others were trying to move the broken branch, the boys found the small opening, ran along the tunnel, and found Mr Mole in a panic because part of his ceiling had fallen down. 'Don't worry,' said Thomas. 'Our Pas and some friends are clearing your front door.

Suddenly, another bigger piece of ceiling crashed down, blocking the passageway and injuring Thomas's foot. 'Dear me, that looks quite bad,' said Mole.

Pa, Uncle Mouse, Squirrel and Rabbit at last moved the broken branch.

When they got inside and found that Thomas was injured, Uncle Mouse carried him back home, while the others helped Mr Mole to put his house in order. He thanked them as they left and asked if any others were in trouble. 'We are not sure yet,' said Squirrel. 'Kingfisher is flying around to find out.'

All that day Mrs Mouse and Sally were busy making hot drinks and helping those who were hurt.

Mr Mole began to realise that his neighbours were kind and helpful and that he ought to be more friendly. So he decided he'd find out how Thomas was getting on. They were pleased to see him and he was glad to find that Thomas was a little better. 'I think you and Timothy were very brave to come to my rescue. Thank you very much,' he said.

Mr Mole then went along to see Timothy and his parents.

'I was wondering what I could do to help any others who are in trouble,' he said.

'How about a carol concert?' said Mrs Mouse. 'I'm sure our children and their friends would like to help and you could make an appeal for gifts.'

'Brilliant!' said Mr Mole. 'There is a piano in the Village Hall where we could rehearse, and we can have the concert outside by the Christmas tree.' 'Oh yes!' cried Sally Mouse. 'We'd love that.'

Very soon, Mr Mole had an excellent choir. They practised until they were perfect.

They put posters round the Village, which read:

GRAND CAROL CONCERT
by the Christmas Tree outside the Hall
on the 23rd.
Everybody welcome — but please bring
a gift for those in need.

The great day came and the crowds arrived, each bringing their gift. As darkness fell, the lights on the Christmas tree started to shine.

Mr Mole sat down at the piano, which had been pushed outside, and the choir gathered around him. As they started to sing, Millie Mouse's squeaky little voice could be heard above the rest, but it all sounded wonderful, and the crowd were amazed at how beautifully Mr Mole played the piano.

After a little while, Mr Mole thanked everybody for coming and bringing their gifts, Then he said 'We would like you all to join in the singing.' As he started to play 'The First Noël' their voices rang out through the trees.

At the end everybody clapped and cheered and someone shouted, 'Three cheers for Mr Mole !' As the crowd made their way home the first big snowflakes of Christmas started to fall.

The Carol Concert had been such a success that there were enough presents for all those in need. Kingfisher had made a long list including Mr Badger, whose shop had been damaged. Whether they were birds or animals, they were all going to be helped to have a happy Christmas.

The Mouse family and friends worked hard, packing parcels to fill a sleigh made by Mr Badger.

Now it was Christmas Eve; the sleigh was ready, the parcels stacked and Kingfisher perched on top checking his list. Mr Mole was ready in his red cloak and hat, looking just like Father Christmas.

Just as Squirrel, Rabbit and Badger began to pull the sleigh, snow started to fall again. 'Happy Christmas !' they all called to each other.

23

The animals and birds who received help were so grateful to everybody and specially to Mr Mole. He spent a happy Christmas Day with Mr and Mrs Mouse and their family. Aunt and Uncle Mouse were there and so was Thomas, who was now almost well again.

When it was time for Mr Mole to leave, he thanked them for giving him such an enjoyable day. As he strolled home, he thought, 'How lucky for me that such a kind, friendly family moved into that house across the stream, because I need never be lonely or unhappy again.'